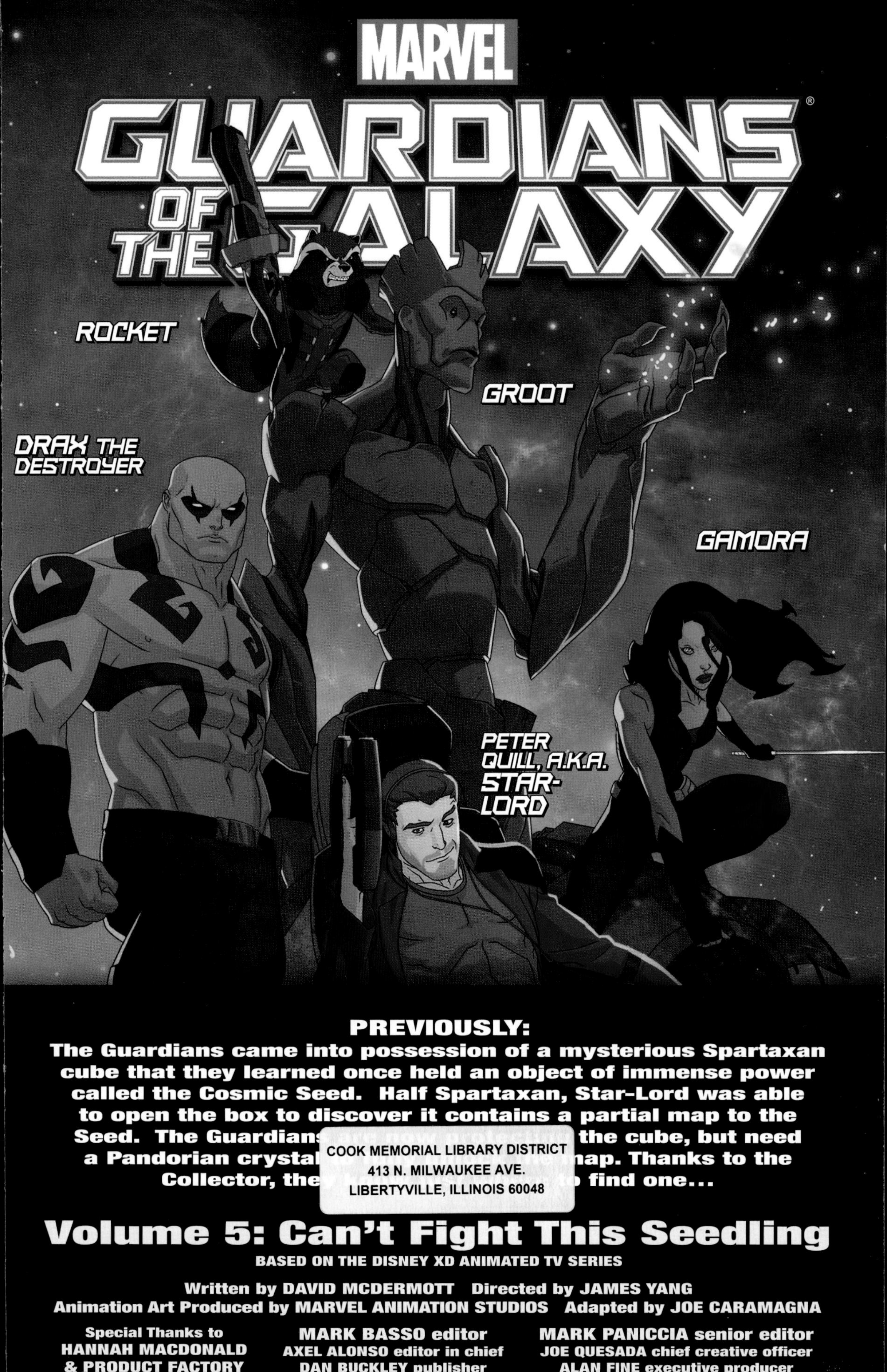
MARVEL
GUARDIANS OF THE GALAXY
ROCKET
GROOT
DRAX THE DESTROYER
GAMORA
PETER QUILL, A.K.A. STAR-LORD

PREVIOUSLY:
The Guardians came into possession of a mysterious Spartaxan cube that they learned once held an object of immense power called the Cosmic Seed. Half Spartaxan, Star-Lord was able to open the box to discover it contains a partial map to the Seed. The Guardians [illegible] the cube, but need a Pandorian crystal [illegible] map. Thanks to the Collector, the[illegible] find one...

Volume 5: Can't Fight This Seedling

BASED ON THE DISNEY XD ANIMATED TV SERIES

Written by DAVID MCDERMOTT Directed by JAMES YANG
Animation Art Produced by MARVEL ANIMATION STUDIOS Adapted by JOE CARAMAGNA

Special Thanks to HANNAH MACDONALD & PRODUCT FACTORY

MARK BASSO editor
AXEL ALONSO editor in chief
DAN BUCKLEY publisher

MARK PANICCIA senior editor
JOE QUESADA chief creative officer
ALAN FINE executive producer

ABDOPUBLISHING.COM

Reinforced library bound edition published in 2018 by Spotlight, a division of ABDO, PO Box 398166, Minneapolis, Minnesota 55439. Spotlight produces high-quality reinforced library bound editions for schools and libraries. Published by agreement with Marvel Characters, Inc.

Printed in the United States of America, North Mankato, Minnesota.
042017
092017

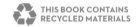

THIS BOOK CONTAINS RECYCLED MATERIALS

marvelkids.com

PUBLISHER'S CATALOGING IN PUBLICATION DATA

Names: McDermott, David ; Caramagna, Joe, authors. | Marvel Animation, illustrator.
Title: Can't fight this seedling / writers: David McDermott ; Joe Caramagna ; art: Marvel Animation.
Description: Reinforced library bound edition. | Minneapolis, Minnesota : Spotlight, 2018. | Series: Guardians of the galaxy ; volume 5
Summary: On a mission to find the next Pandorian Crystal, the Guardians encounter a race of aliens that are under attack by rock-like Rexians and help fight them off, but Groot becomes infected with the same fungus that possesses the Rexians.
Identifiers: LCCN 2017931210 | ISBN 9781532140747 (lib. bdg.)
Subjects: LCSH: Superheroes--Juvenile fiction. | Adventure and adventurers--Juvenile fiction. | Comic books, strips, etc.--Juvenile fiction. | Graphic novels--Juvenile fiction.
Classification: DDC 741.5--dc23
LC record available at https://lccn.loc.gov/2017931210

ABDO

Spotlight

A Division of ABDO
abdopublishing.com

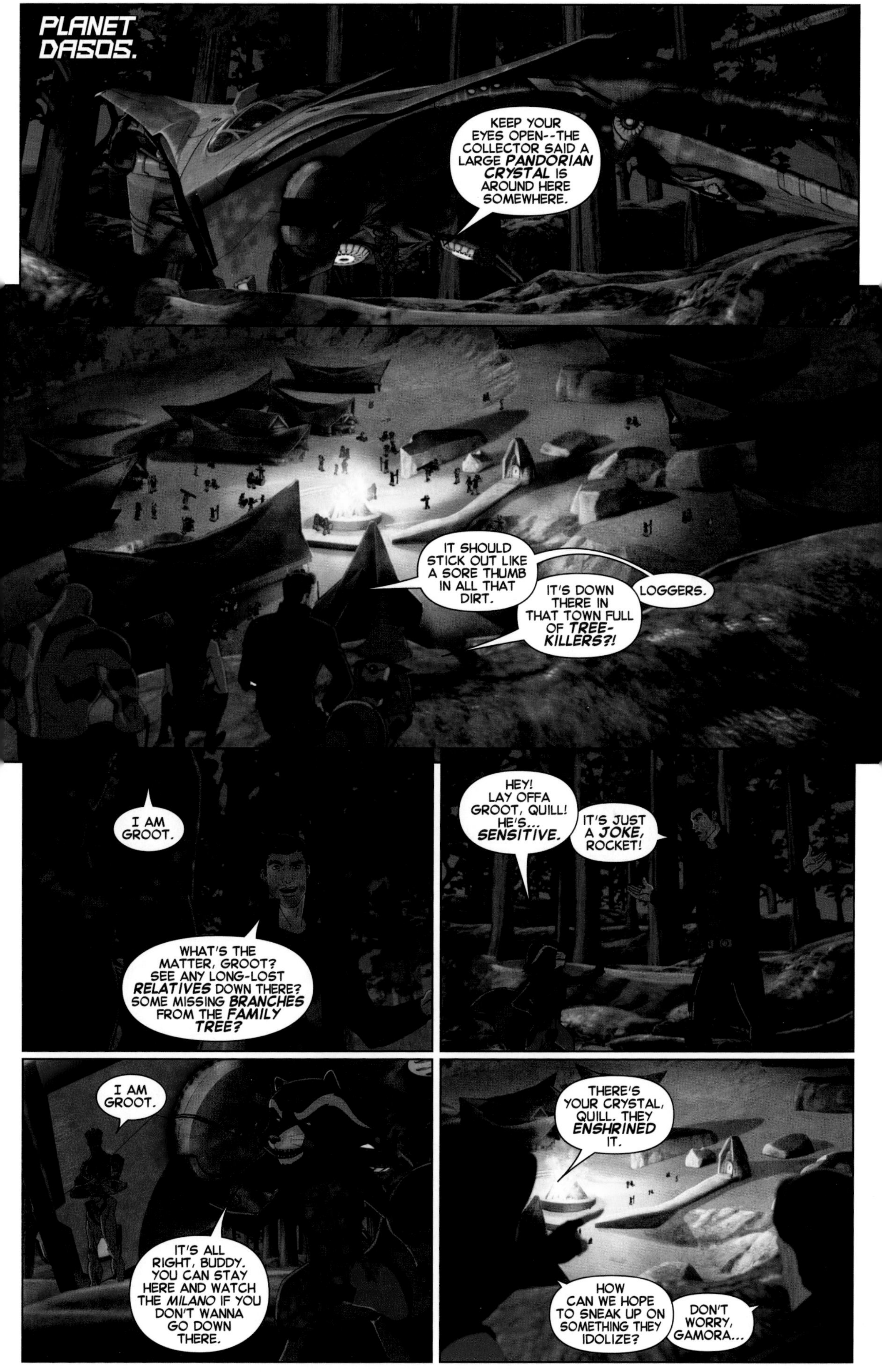
PLANET DASOS.
KEEP YOUR EYES OPEN--THE COLLECTOR SAID A LARGE PANDORIAN CRYSTAL IS AROUND HERE SOMEWHERE.
IT SHOULD STICK OUT LIKE A SORE THUMB IN ALL THAT DIRT.
IT'S DOWN THERE IN THAT TOWN FULL OF TREE-KILLERS?!
LOGGERS.
I AM GROOT.
WHAT'S THE MATTER, GROOT? SEE ANY LONG-LOST RELATIVES DOWN THERE? SOME MISSING BRANCHES FROM THE FAMILY TREE?
HEY! LAY OFFA GROOT, QUILL! HE'S... SENSITIVE.
IT'S JUST A JOKE, ROCKET!
I AM GROOT.
IT'S ALL RIGHT, BUDDY. YOU CAN STAY HERE AND WATCH THE MILANO IF YOU DON'T WANNA GO DOWN THERE.
THERE'S YOUR CRYSTAL, QUILL. THEY ENSHRINED IT.
HOW CAN WE HOPE TO SNEAK UP ON SOMETHING THEY IDOLIZE?
DON'T WORRY, GAMORA...

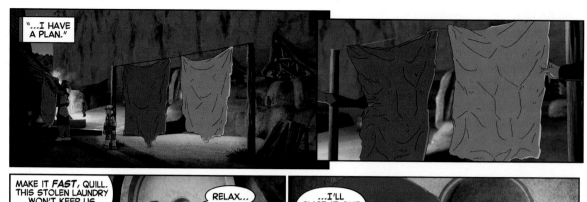

"...I HAVE A PLAN."

MAKE IT **FAST**, QUILL. THIS STOLEN LAUNDRY WON'T KEEP US HIDDEN FOR LONG.

RELAX...

...I'LL SLICE IT OUT BEFORE YOU CAN SAY--

INTRUDER!

WHAT SORT OF **BLADE** IS THAT?

OH, HEY, WE... UH--

WAIT-- **WHAT?!**

WHAT DO YOU **WANT** FOR IT?

YOU MEAN THIS **LITTLE**--

OH! ERR, IT'S QUITE **VALUABLE**, ACTUALLY.

IT'S PROBABLY WORTH AS MUCH AS YOUR **CRYSTAL.**

THEN IT'S A **TRADE.** THE BLADE FOR THE CRYSTAL.

I CAN'T BELIEVE THAT CHUMP TRADED THE CRYSTAL FOR A **POCKET-KNIFE!**

I CAN'T BELIEVE THAT SIMPLETON TRADED THIS **AMAZING BLADE** FOR THAT WORTHLESS HUNK OF ROCK!

I AM GROOT!

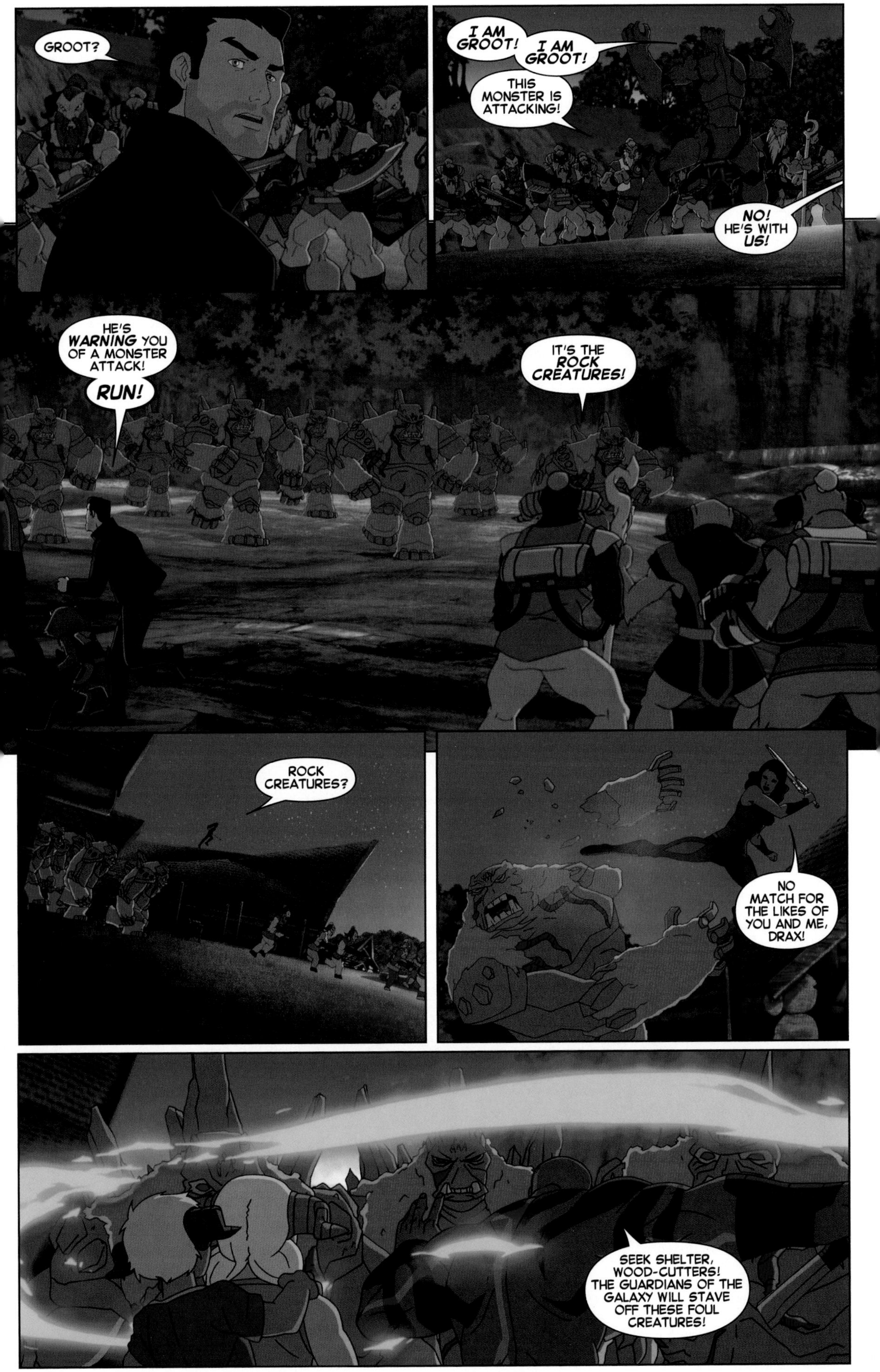
GROOT?
I AM GROOT!
I AM GROOT!
THIS MONSTER IS ATTACKING!
NO! HE'S WITH US!
HE'S WARNING YOU OF A MONSTER ATTACK!
RUN!
IT'S THE ROCK CREATURES!
ROCK CREATURES?
NO MATCH FOR THE LIKES OF YOU AND ME, DRAX!
SEEK SHELTER, WOOD-CUTTERS! THE GUARDIANS OF THE GALAXY WILL STAVE OFF THESE FOUL CREATURES!

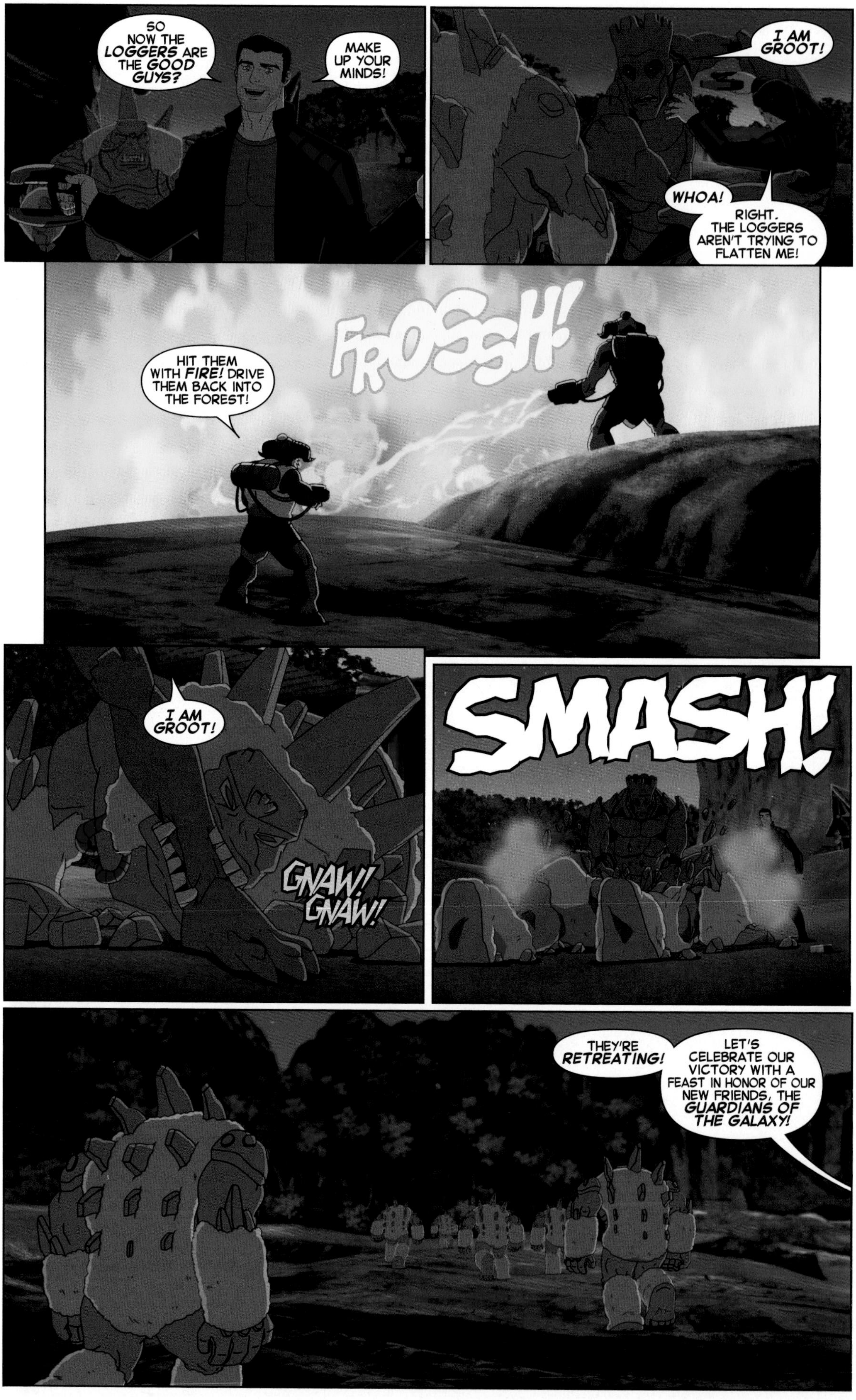
SO NOW THE LOGGERS ARE THE GOOD GUYS?
MAKE UP YOUR MINDS!
I AM GROOT!
WHOA!
RIGHT. THE LOGGERS AREN'T TRYING TO FLATTEN ME!
FROSSH!
HIT THEM WITH FIRE! DRIVE THEM BACK INTO THE FOREST!
I AM GROOT!
GNAW! GNAW!
SMASH!
THEY'RE RETREATING!
LET'S CELEBRATE OUR VICTORY WITH A FEAST IN HONOR OF OUR NEW FRIENDS, THE GUARDIANS OF THE GALAXY!

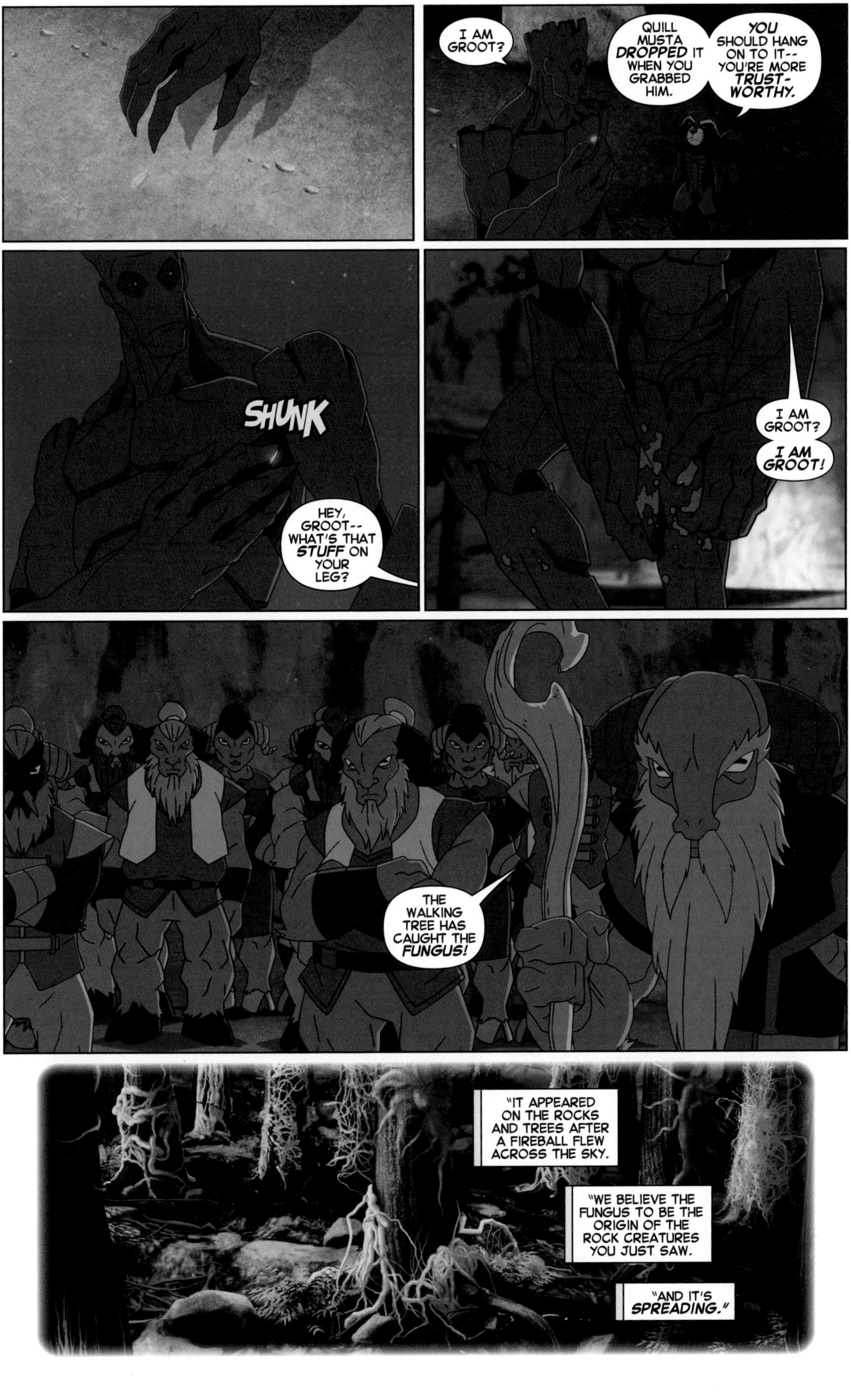

I AM GROOT?
QUILL MUSTA DROPPED IT WHEN YOU GRABBED HIM.
YOU SHOULD HANG ON TO IT-- YOU'RE MORE TRUST-WORTHY.
SHUNK
HEY, GROOT-- WHAT'S THAT STUFF ON YOUR LEG?
I AM GROOT?
I AM GROOT!
THE WALKING TREE HAS CAUGHT THE FUNGUS!
"IT APPEARED ON THE ROCKS AND TREES AFTER A FIREBALL FLEW ACROSS THE SKY.
"WE BELIEVE THE FUNGUS TO BE THE ORIGIN OF THE ROCK CREATURES YOU JUST SAW.
"AND IT'S SPREADING."

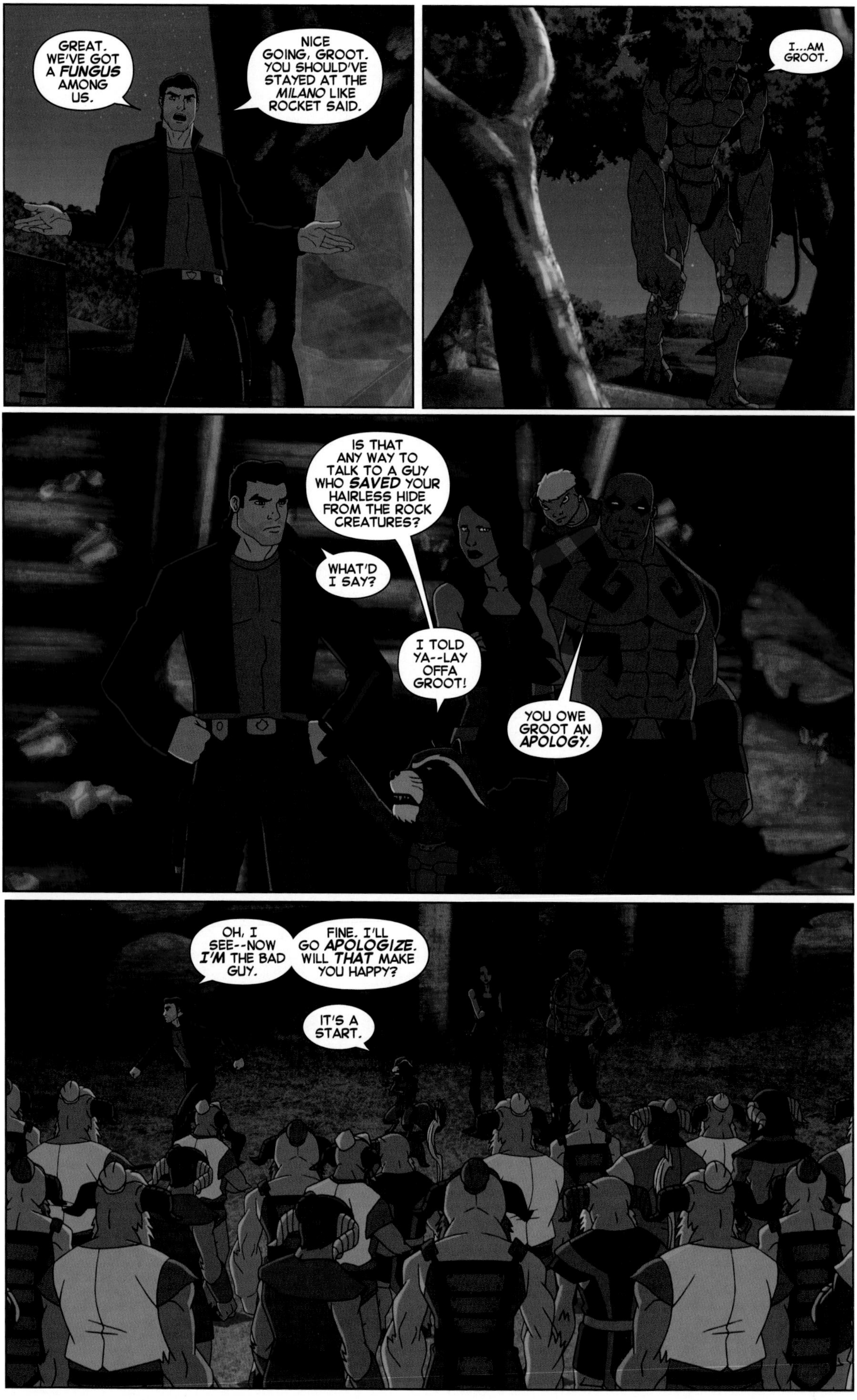
GREAT. WE'VE GOT A *FUNGUS* AMONG US.
NICE GOING, GROOT. YOU SHOULD'VE STAYED AT THE *MILANO* LIKE ROCKET SAID.
I...AM GROOT.
IS THAT ANY WAY TO TALK TO A GUY WHO **SAVED** YOUR HAIRLESS HIDE FROM THE ROCK CREATURES?
WHAT'D I SAY?
I TOLD YA--LAY OFFA GROOT!
YOU OWE GROOT AN *APOLOGY.*
OH, I SEE--NOW *I'M* THE BAD GUY.
FINE. I'LL GO *APOLOGIZE.* WILL *THAT* MAKE YOU HAPPY?
IT'S A START.

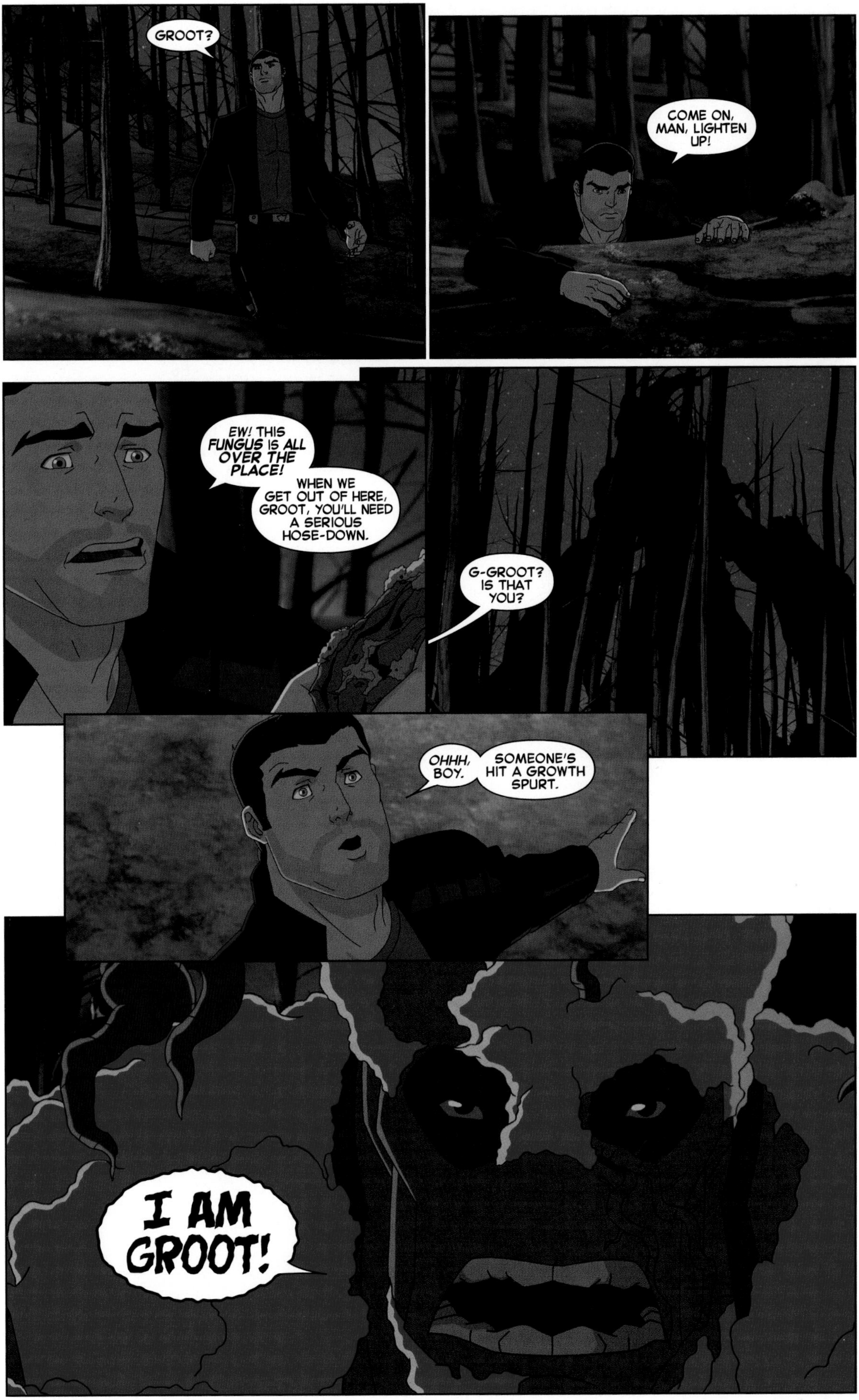
GROOT?
COME ON, MAN, LIGHTEN UP!
EW! THIS FUNGUS IS ALL OVER THE PLACE!
WHEN WE GET OUT OF HERE, GROOT, YOU'LL NEED A SERIOUS HOSE-DOWN.
G-GROOT? IS THAT YOU?
OHHH, BOY.
SOMEONE'S HIT A GROWTH SPURT.
I AM GROOT!

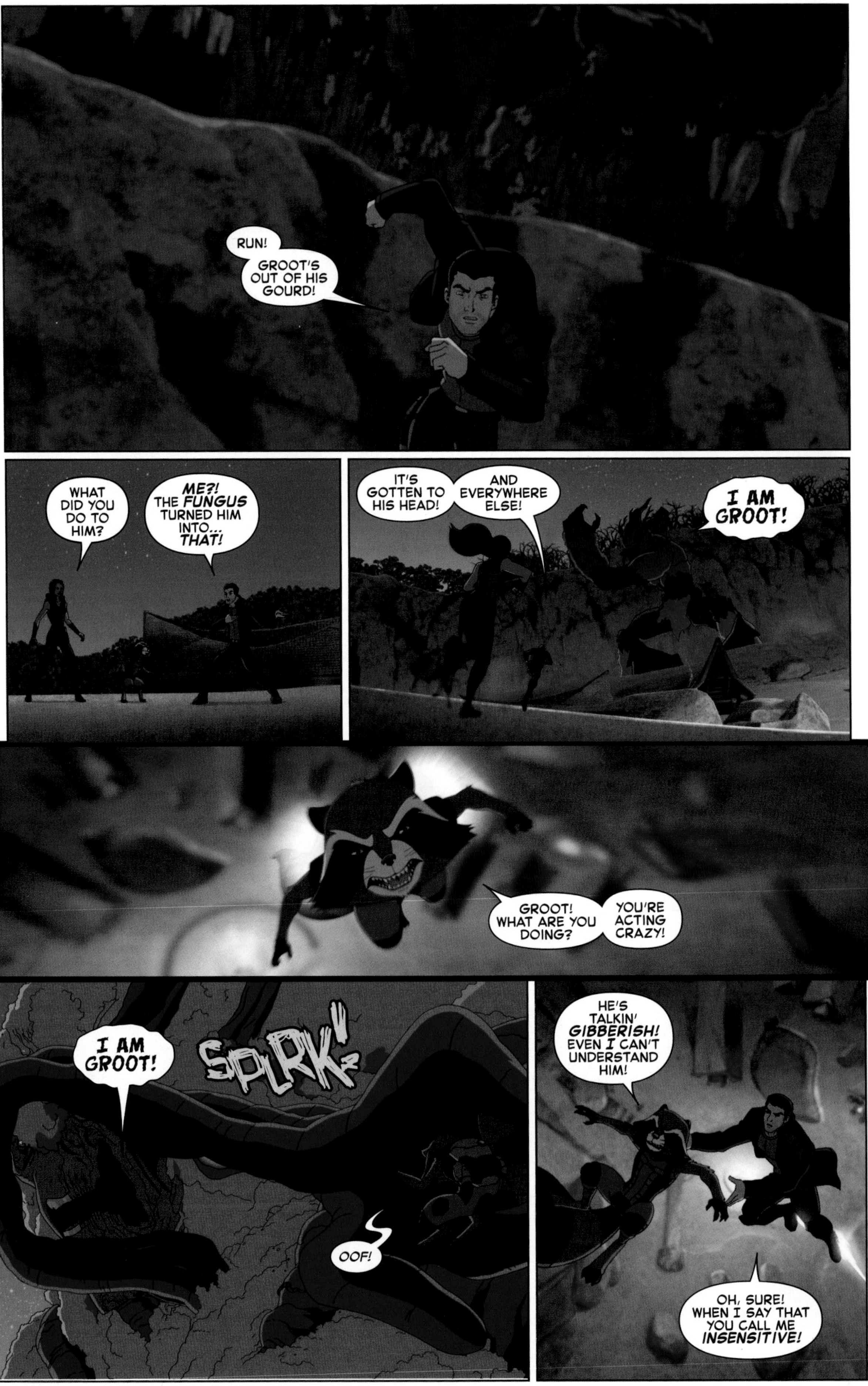
RUN!
GROOT'S OUT OF HIS GOURD!
WHAT DID YOU DO TO HIM?
ME?! THE FUNGUS TURNED HIM INTO... THAT!
IT'S GOTTEN TO HIS HEAD!
AND EVERYWHERE ELSE!
I AM GROOT!
GROOT! WHAT ARE YOU DOING?
YOU'RE ACTING CRAZY!
I AM GROOT!
SPLRK!
OOF!
HE'S TALKIN' GIBBERISH! EVEN I CAN'T UNDERSTAND HIM!
OH, SURE! WHEN I SAY THAT YOU CALL ME INSENSITIVE!

I'VE GOT AN IDEA ON HOW TO SLOW HIM DOWN.

FRKK!

GREAT. ANOTHER ONE OF YOUR *IDEAS*.

YOU CAN'T WALK IF YOUR FEET ARE *FROZEN* TO THE GROUND, RIGHT?

TIMBER!

CRASH!

I AM GROOT!

HE'S OUT COLD. BUT HE WON'T BE OUT FOR LONG!

IF THE FUNGUS *CONTROLS* HIM--

--WE MUST *REMOVE* IT!

DEET!

EASIER SAID THAN DONE, DRAX.

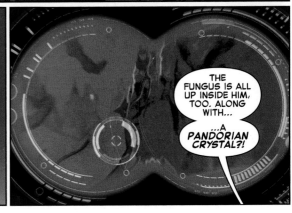

THE FUNGUS IS ALL UP INSIDE HIM, TOO. ALONG WITH...

...A *PANDORIAN CRYSTAL?!*

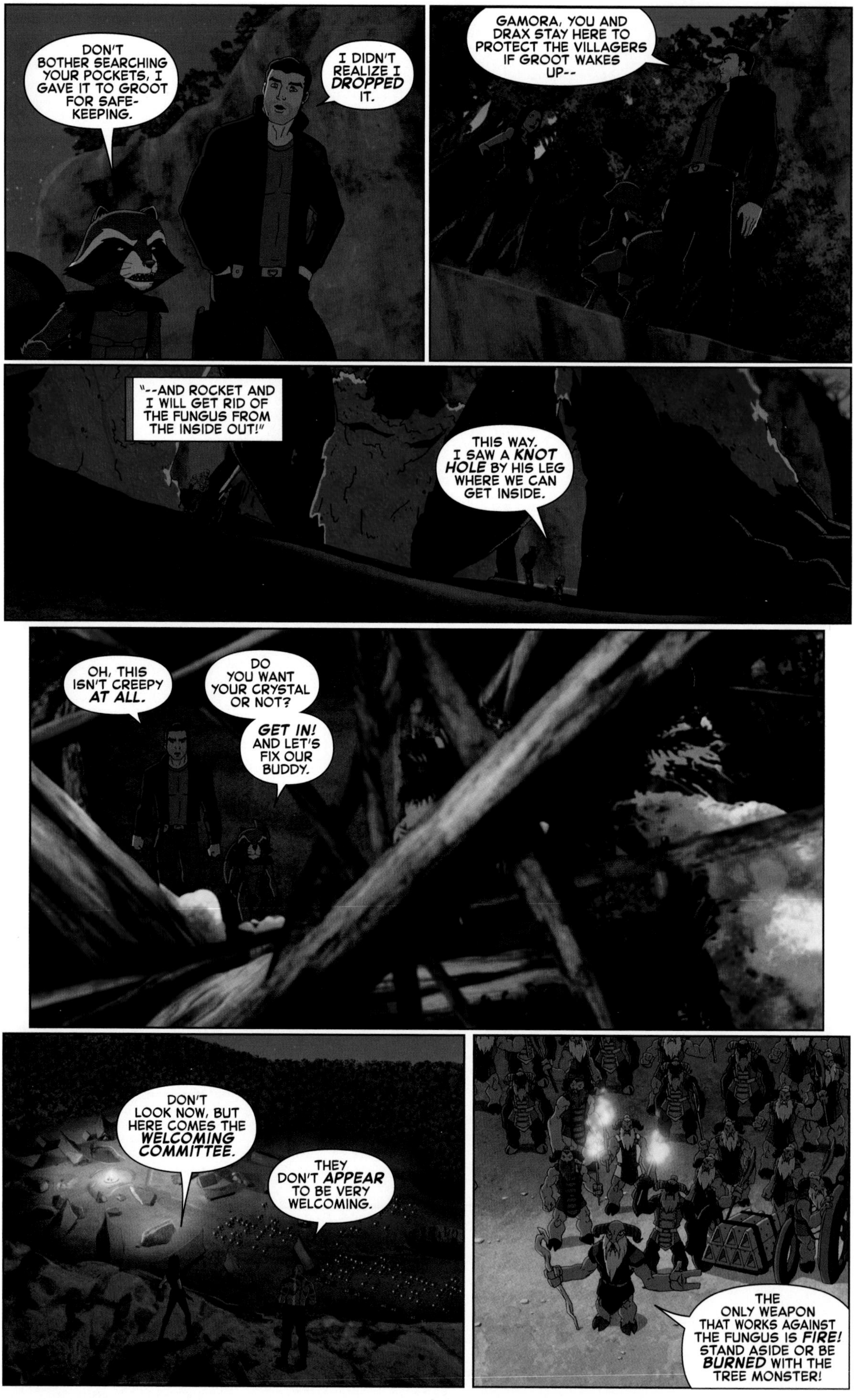
DON'T BOTHER SEARCHING YOUR POCKETS, I GAVE IT TO GROOT FOR SAFE-KEEPING.
I DIDN'T REALIZE I DROPPED IT.
GAMORA, YOU AND DRAX STAY HERE TO PROTECT THE VILLAGERS IF GROOT WAKES UP--
"--AND ROCKET AND I WILL GET RID OF THE FUNGUS FROM THE INSIDE OUT!"
THIS WAY. I SAW A KNOT HOLE BY HIS LEG WHERE WE CAN GET INSIDE.
OH, THIS ISN'T CREEPY AT ALL.
DO YOU WANT YOUR CRYSTAL OR NOT?
GET IN! AND LET'S FIX OUR BUDDY.
DON'T LOOK NOW, BUT HERE COMES THE WELCOMING COMMITTEE.
THEY DON'T APPEAR TO BE VERY WELCOMING.
THE ONLY WEAPON THAT WORKS AGAINST THE FUNGUS IS FIRE! STAND ASIDE OR BE BURNED WITH THE TREE MONSTER!

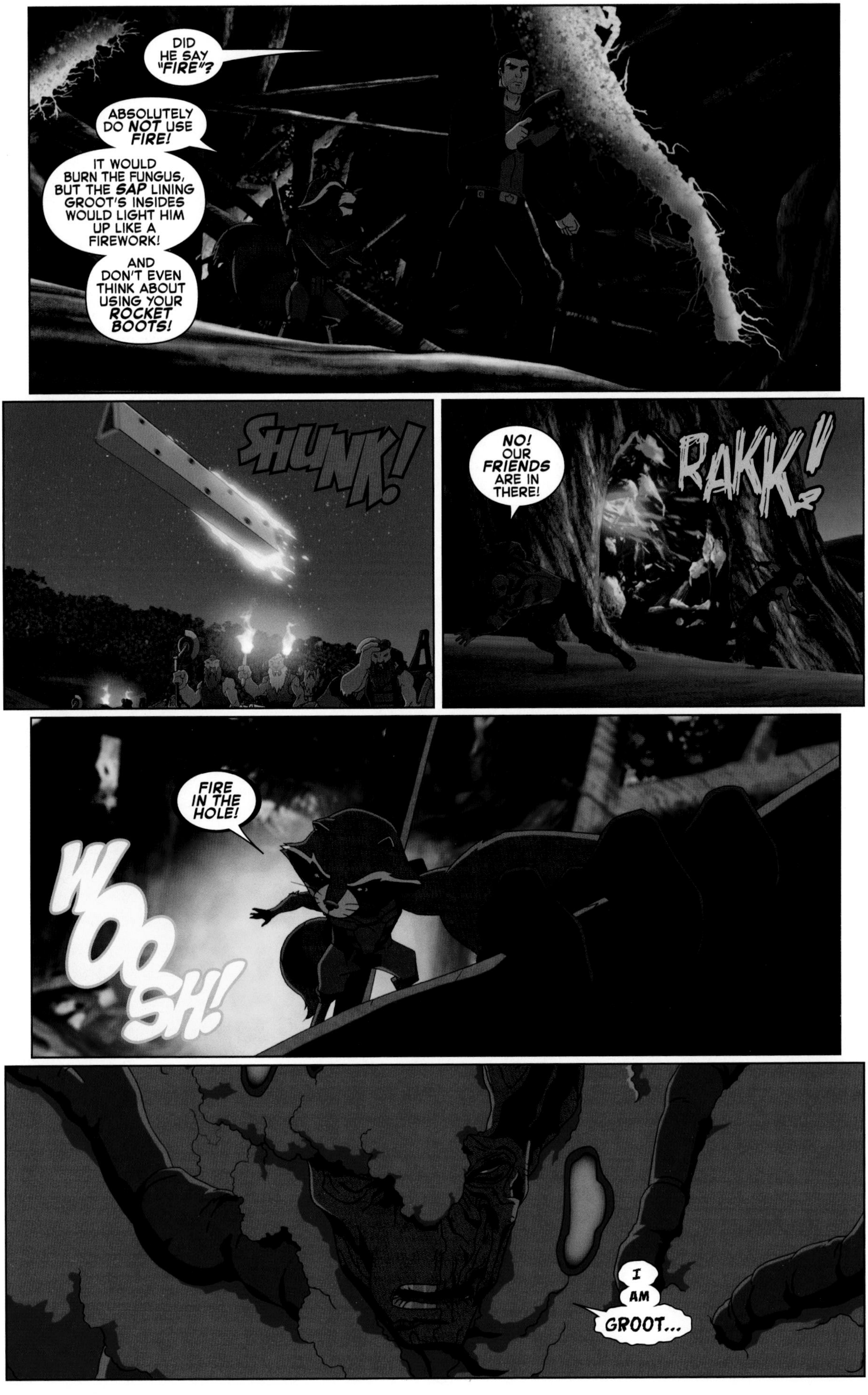
DID HE SAY "FIRE"?
ABSOLUTELY DO NOT USE FIRE!
IT WOULD BURN THE FUNGUS, BUT THE SAP LINING GROOT'S INSIDES WOULD LIGHT HIM UP LIKE A FIREWORK!
AND DON'T EVEN THINK ABOUT USING YOUR ROCKET BOOTS!
SHUNK!
NO! OUR FRIENDS ARE IN THERE!
RAKK!
FIRE IN THE HOLE!
WOOOSH!
I AM GROOT...

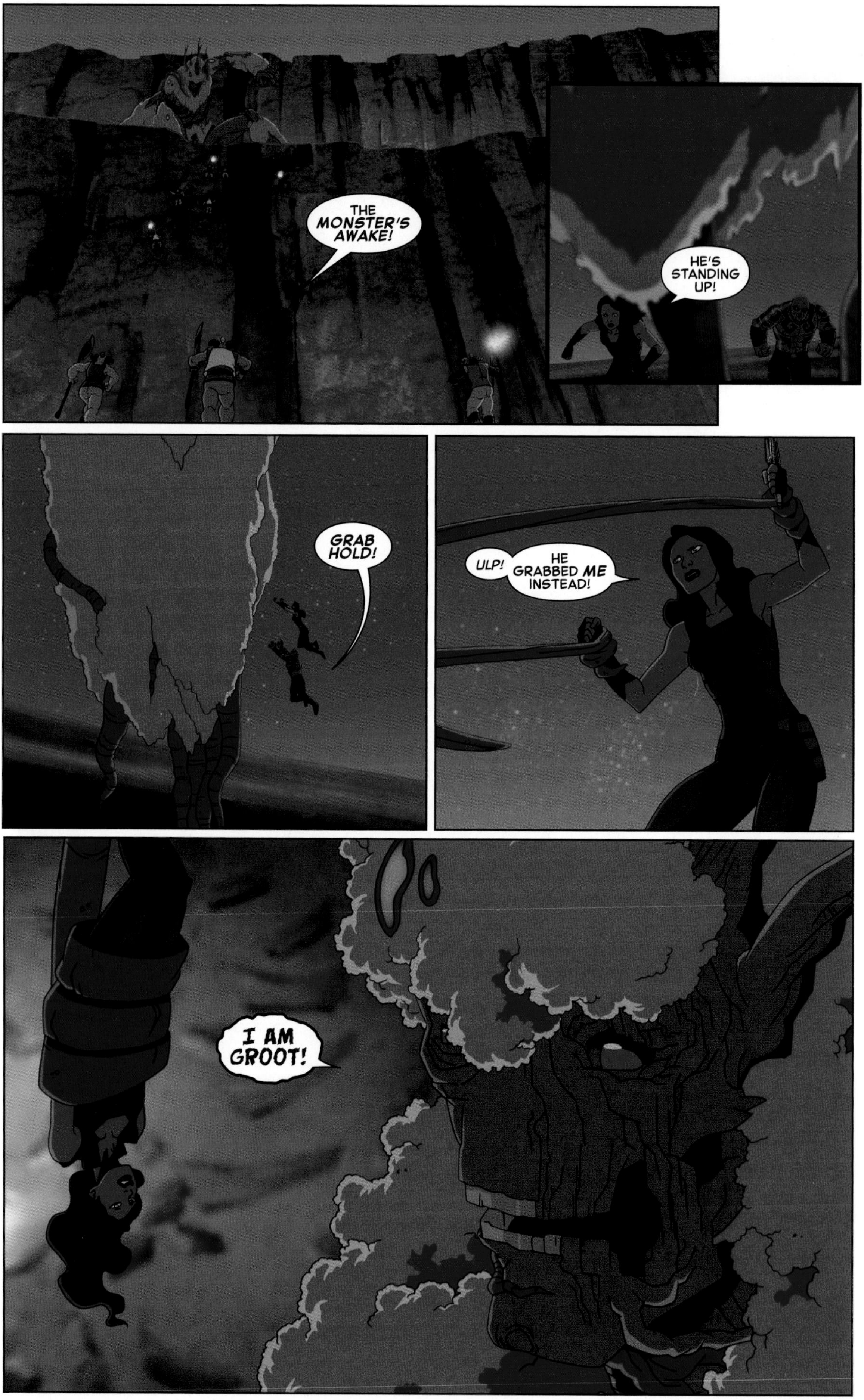
THE MONSTER'S AWAKE!
HE'S STANDING UP!
GRAB HOLD!
ULP!
HE GRABBED ME INSTEAD!
I AM GROOT!

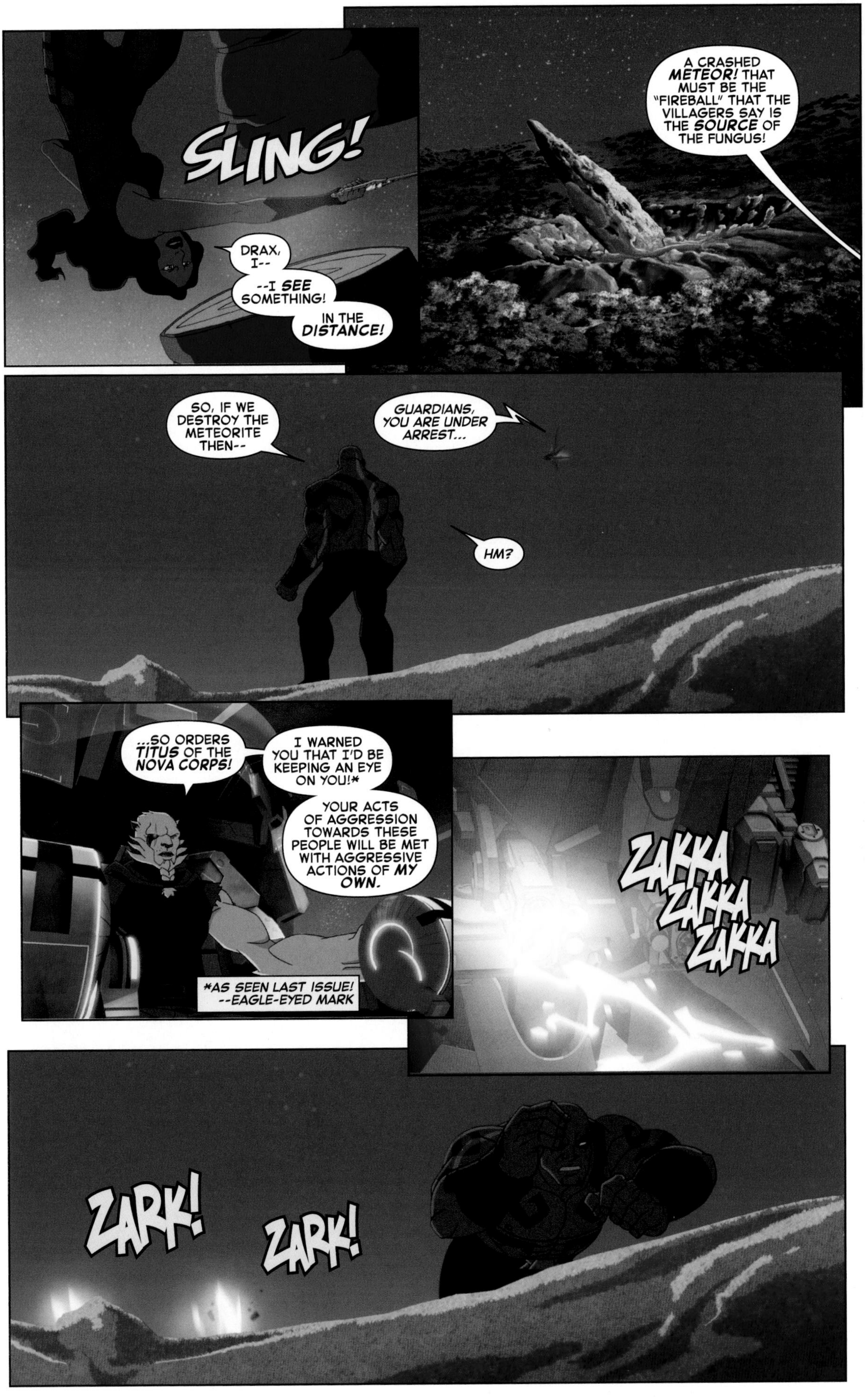
SLING!
DRAX, I--
--I SEE SOMETHING!
IN THE DISTANCE!
A CRASHED METEOR! THAT MUST BE THE "FIREBALL" THAT THE VILLAGERS SAY IS THE SOURCE OF THE FUNGUS!
SO, IF WE DESTROY THE METEORITE THEN--
GUARDIANS, YOU ARE UNDER ARREST...
HM?
...SO ORDERS TITUS OF THE NOVA CORPS!
I WARNED YOU THAT I'D BE KEEPING AN EYE ON YOU!*
YOUR ACTS OF AGGRESSION TOWARDS THESE PEOPLE WILL BE MET WITH AGGRESSIVE ACTIONS OF MY OWN.
*AS SEEN LAST ISSUE! --EAGLE-EYED MARK
ZAKKA ZAKKA ZAKKA
ZARK!
ZARK!

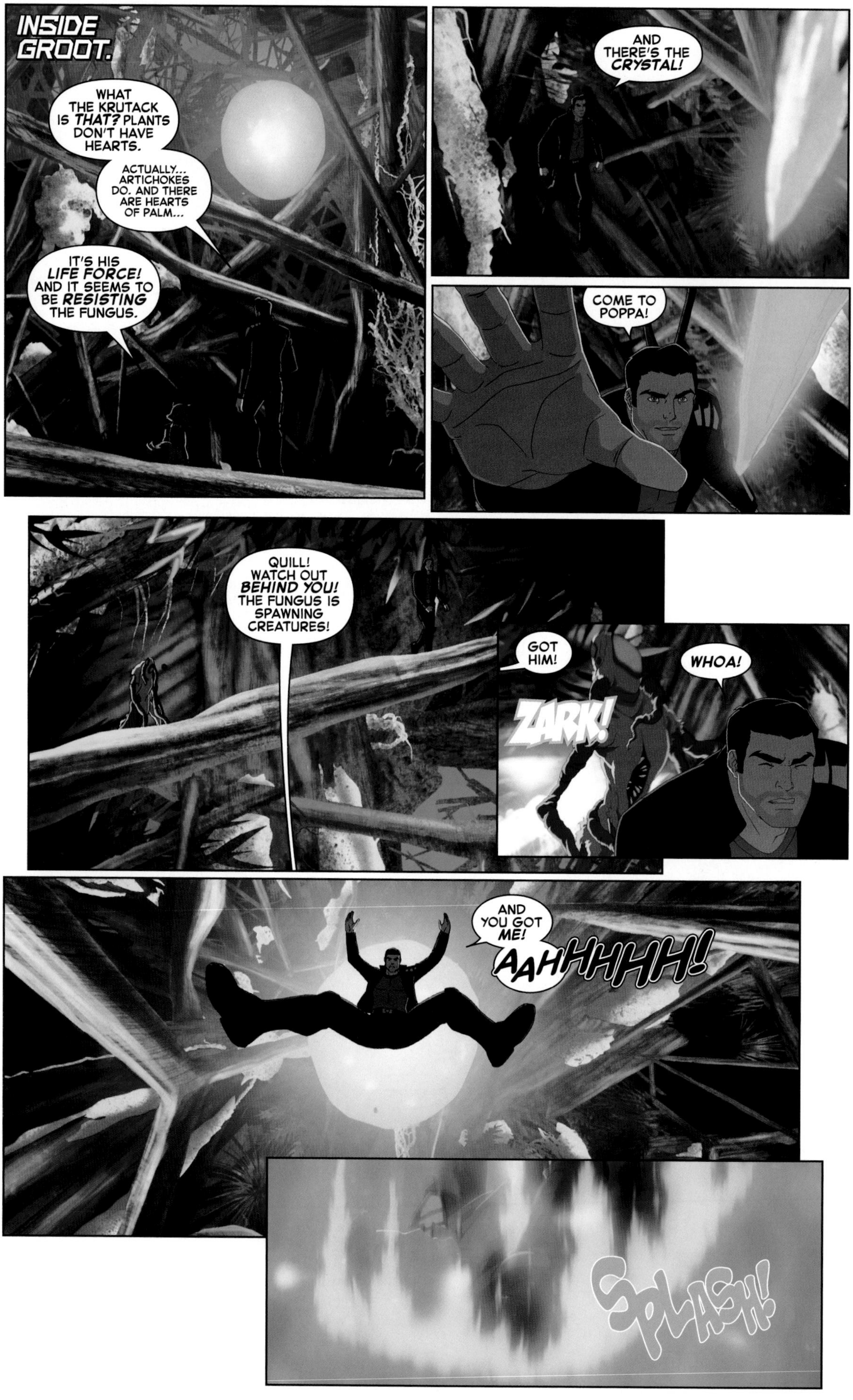
INSIDE GROOT.
WHAT THE KRUTACK IS THAT? PLANTS DON'T HAVE HEARTS.
ACTUALLY... ARTICHOKES DO. AND THERE ARE HEARTS OF PALM...
IT'S HIS LIFE FORCE! AND IT SEEMS TO BE RESISTING THE FUNGUS.
AND THERE'S THE CRYSTAL!
COME TO POPPA!
QUILL! WATCH OUT BEHIND YOU! THE FUNGUS IS SPAWNING CREATURES!
GOT HIM!
WHOA!
ZARK!
AND YOU GOT ME!
AAHHHHH!
SPLASH!

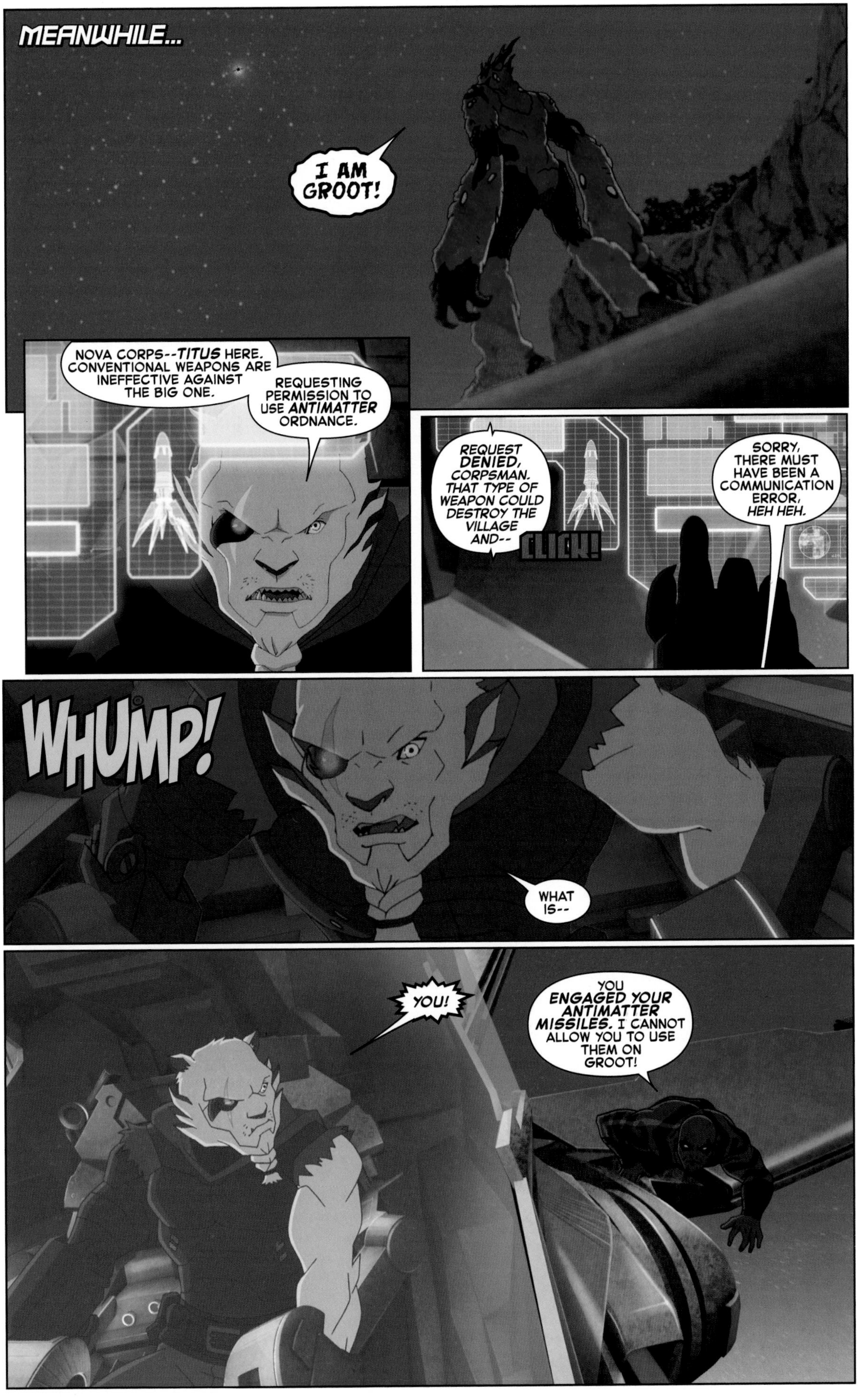
MEANWHILE...
I AM GROOT!
NOVA CORPS--*TITUS* HERE. CONVENTIONAL WEAPONS ARE INEFFECTIVE AGAINST THE BIG ONE.
REQUESTING PERMISSION TO USE *ANTIMATTER* ORDNANCE.
REQUEST **DENIED**, CORPSMAN. THAT TYPE OF WEAPON COULD DESTROY THE VILLAGE AND--
CLICK!
SORRY, THERE MUST HAVE BEEN A COMMUNICATION ERROR, *HEH HEH.*
WHUMP!
WHAT IS--
YOU!
YOU **ENGAGED YOUR *ANTIMATTER MISSILES.*** I CANNOT ALLOW YOU TO USE THEM ON GROOT!

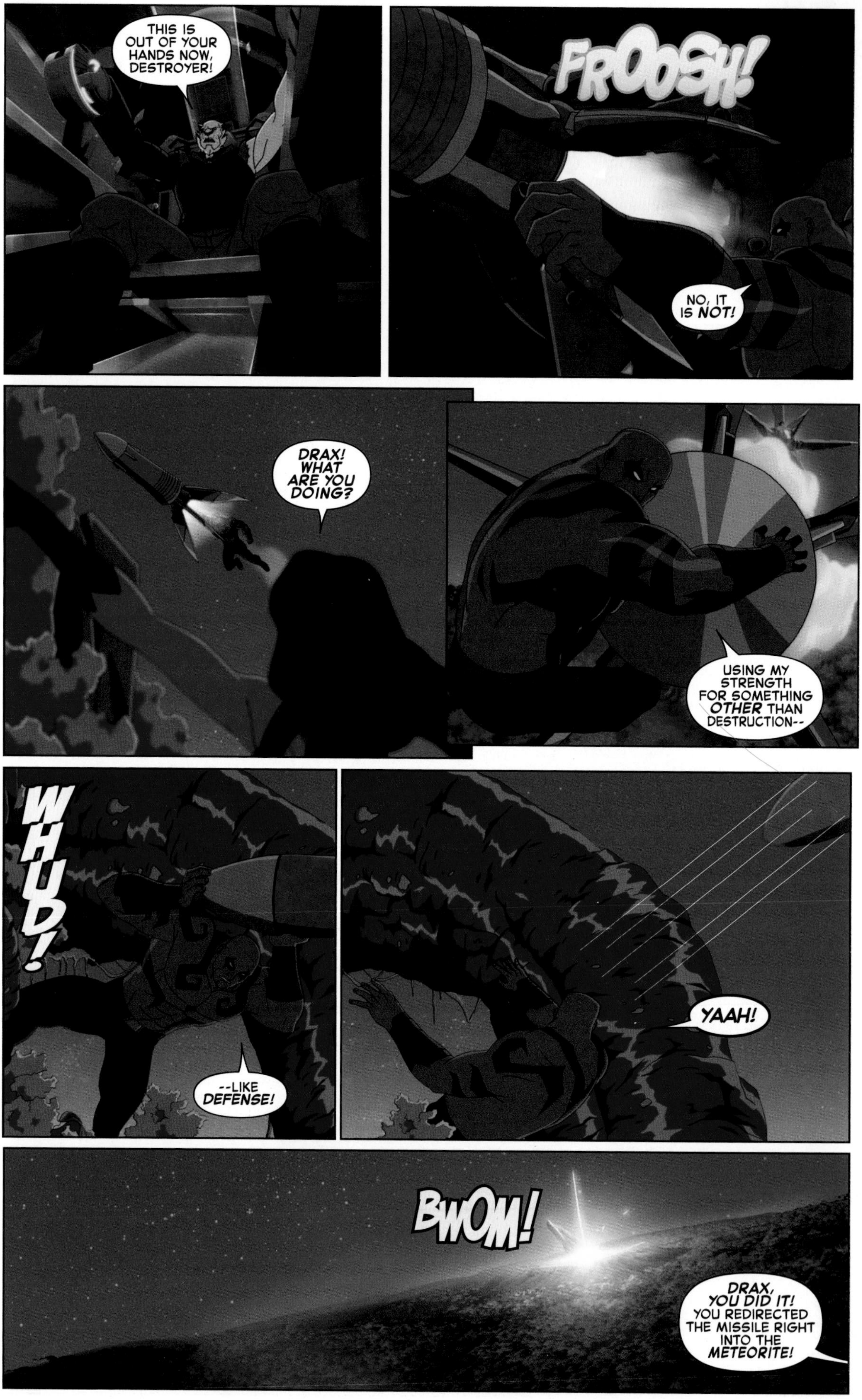
THIS IS OUT OF YOUR HANDS NOW, DESTROYER!
FROOSH!
NO, IT IS NOT!
DRAX! WHAT ARE YOU DOING?
USING MY STRENGTH FOR SOMETHING OTHER THAN DESTRUCTION--
WHUD!
--LIKE DEFENSE!
YAAH!
BWOM!
DRAX, YOU DID IT! YOU REDIRECTED THE MISSILE RIGHT INTO THE METEORITE!

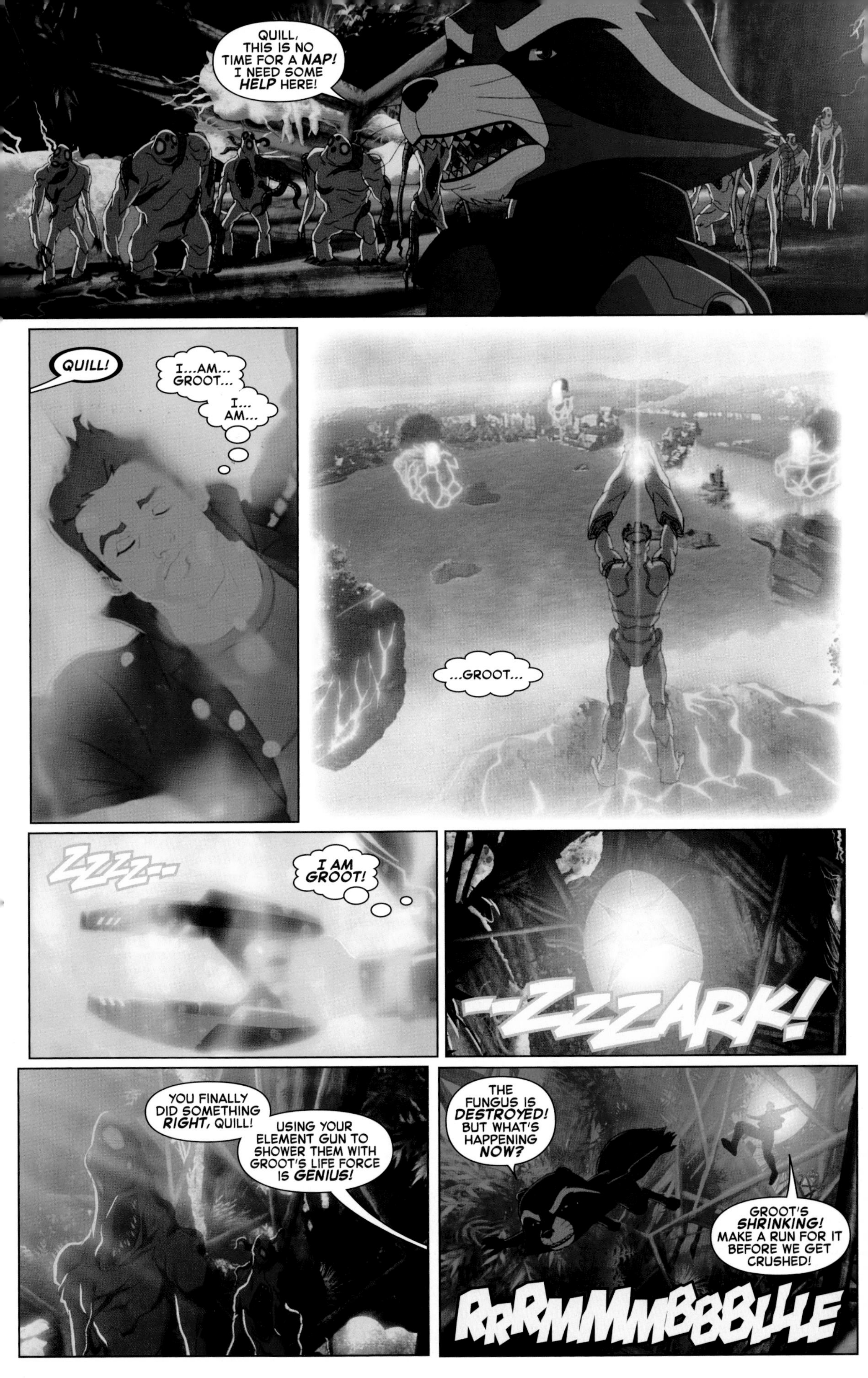
QUILL, THIS IS NO TIME FOR A NAP! I NEED SOME HELP HERE!
QUILL!
I...AM... GROOT... I... AM...
...GROOT...
ZZZZ--
I AM GROOT!
--ZZZARK!
YOU FINALLY DID SOMETHING RIGHT, QUILL!
USING YOUR ELEMENT GUN TO SHOWER THEM WITH GROOT'S LIFE FORCE IS GENIUS!
THE FUNGUS IS DESTROYED! BUT WHAT'S HAPPENING NOW?
GROOT'S SHRINKING! MAKE A RUN FOR IT BEFORE WE GET CRUSHED!
RRRMMMMBBBLLLE

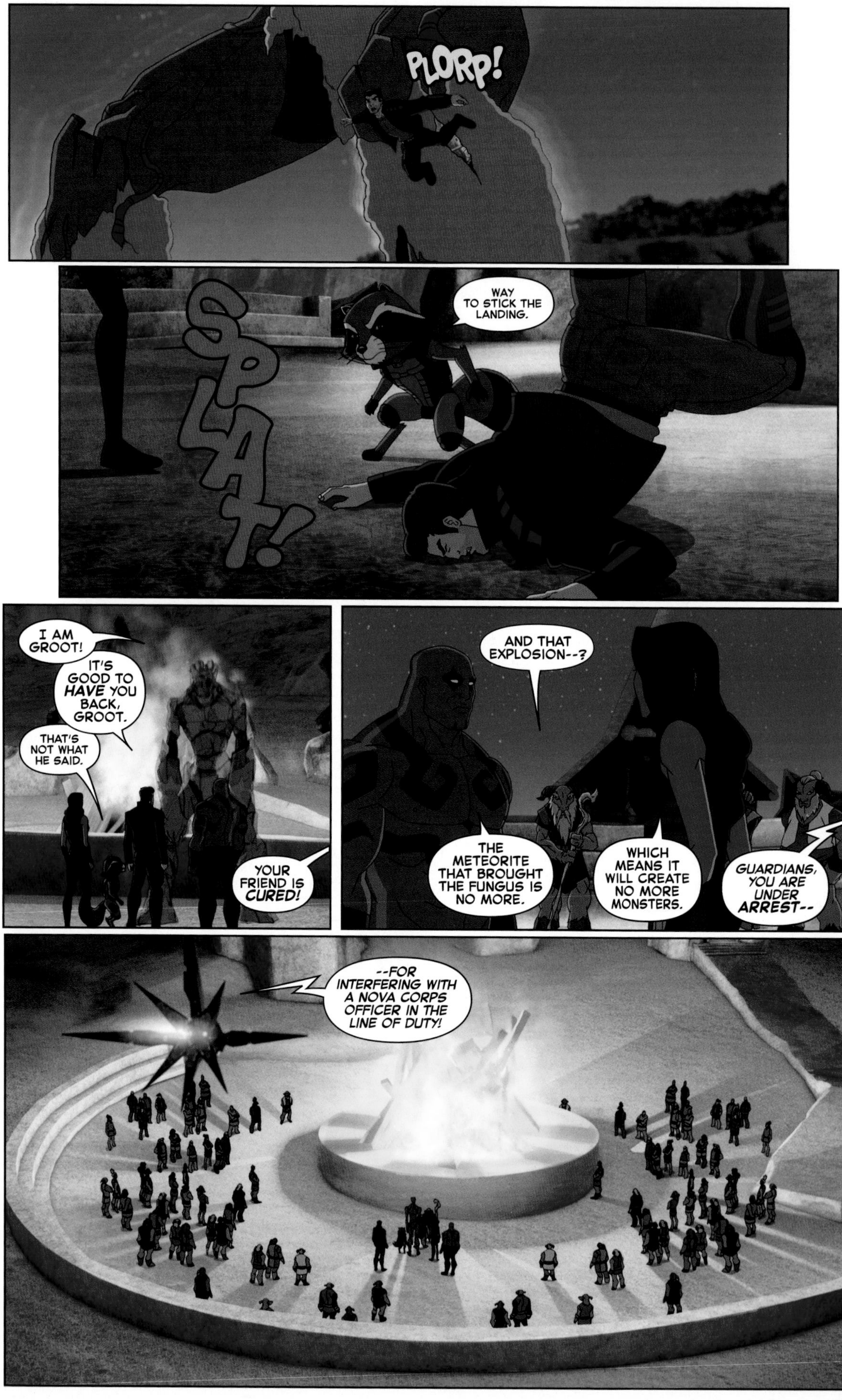
PLORP!
WAY TO STICK THE LANDING.
SPLAT!
I AM GROOT!
IT'S GOOD TO HAVE YOU BACK, GROOT.
THAT'S NOT WHAT HE SAID.
YOUR FRIEND IS CURED!
AND THAT EXPLOSION--?
THE METEORITE THAT BROUGHT THE FUNGUS IS NO MORE.
WHICH MEANS IT WILL CREATE NO MORE MONSTERS.
GUARDIANS, YOU ARE UNDER ARREST--
--FOR INTERFERING WITH A NOVA CORPS OFFICER IN THE LINE OF DUTY!

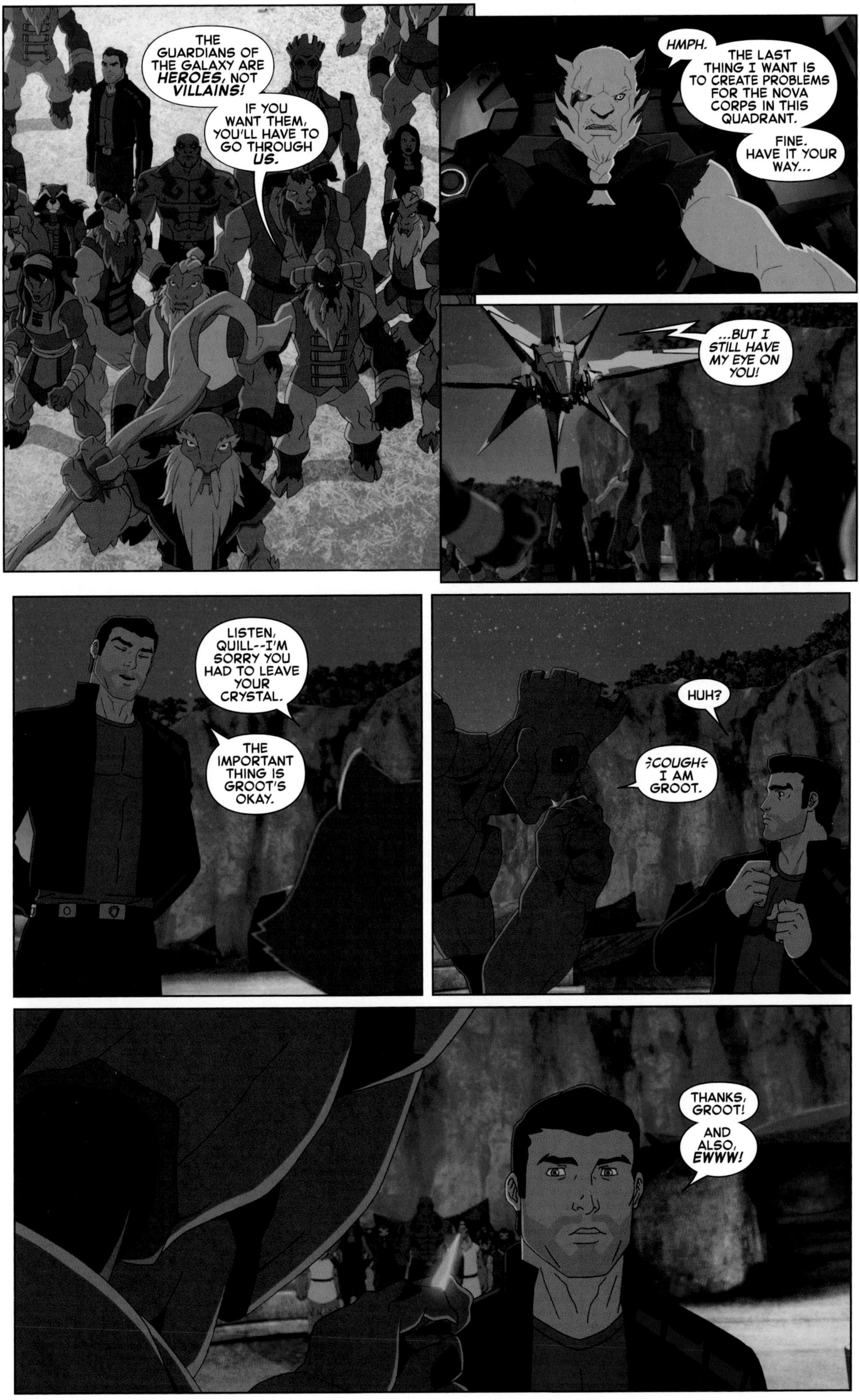
THE GUARDIANS OF THE GALAXY ARE HEROES, NOT VILLAINS!
IF YOU WANT THEM, YOU'LL HAVE TO GO THROUGH US.
HMPH.
THE LAST THING I WANT IS TO CREATE PROBLEMS FOR THE NOVA CORPS IN THIS QUADRANT.
FINE. HAVE IT YOUR WAY...
...BUT I STILL HAVE MY EYE ON YOU!
LISTEN, QUILL--I'M SORRY YOU HAD TO LEAVE YOUR CRYSTAL.
THE IMPORTANT THING IS GROOT'S OKAY.
HUH?
COUGH I AM GROOT.
THANKS, GROOT!
AND ALSO, EWWW!

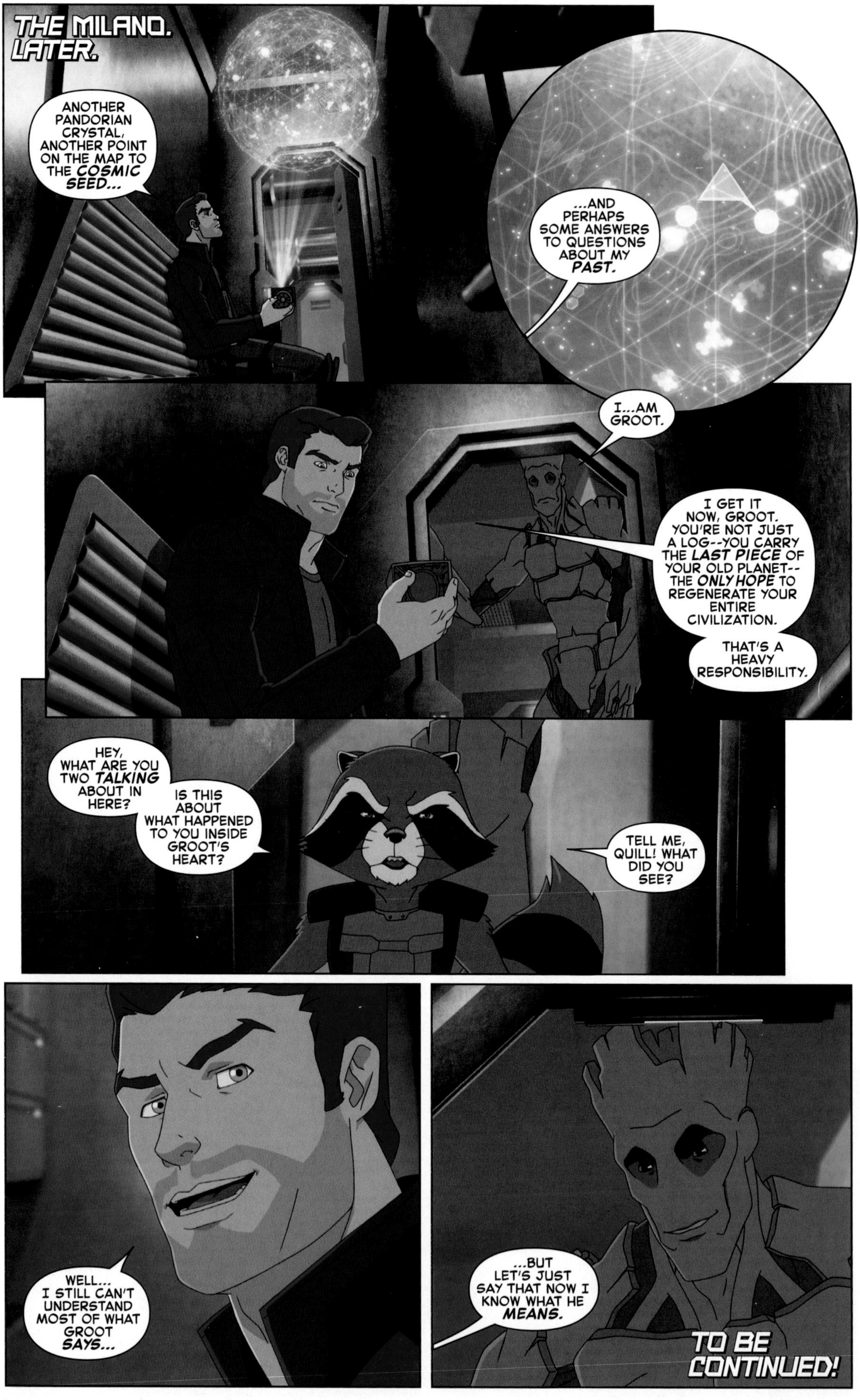
THE MILANO. LATER.
ANOTHER PANDORIAN CRYSTAL, ANOTHER POINT ON THE MAP TO THE COSMIC SEED...
...AND PERHAPS SOME ANSWERS TO QUESTIONS ABOUT MY PAST.
I...AM GROOT.
I GET IT NOW, GROOT. YOU'RE NOT JUST A LOG--YOU CARRY THE LAST PIECE OF YOUR OLD PLANET--THE ONLY HOPE TO REGENERATE YOUR ENTIRE CIVILIZATION.
THAT'S A HEAVY RESPONSIBILITY.
HEY, WHAT ARE YOU TWO TALKING ABOUT IN HERE?
IS THIS ABOUT WHAT HAPPENED TO YOU INSIDE GROOT'S HEART?
TELL ME, QUILL! WHAT DID YOU SEE?
WELL... I STILL CAN'T UNDERSTAND MOST OF WHAT GROOT SAYS...
...BUT LET'S JUST SAY THAT NOW I KNOW WHAT HE MEANS.
TO BE CONTINUED!

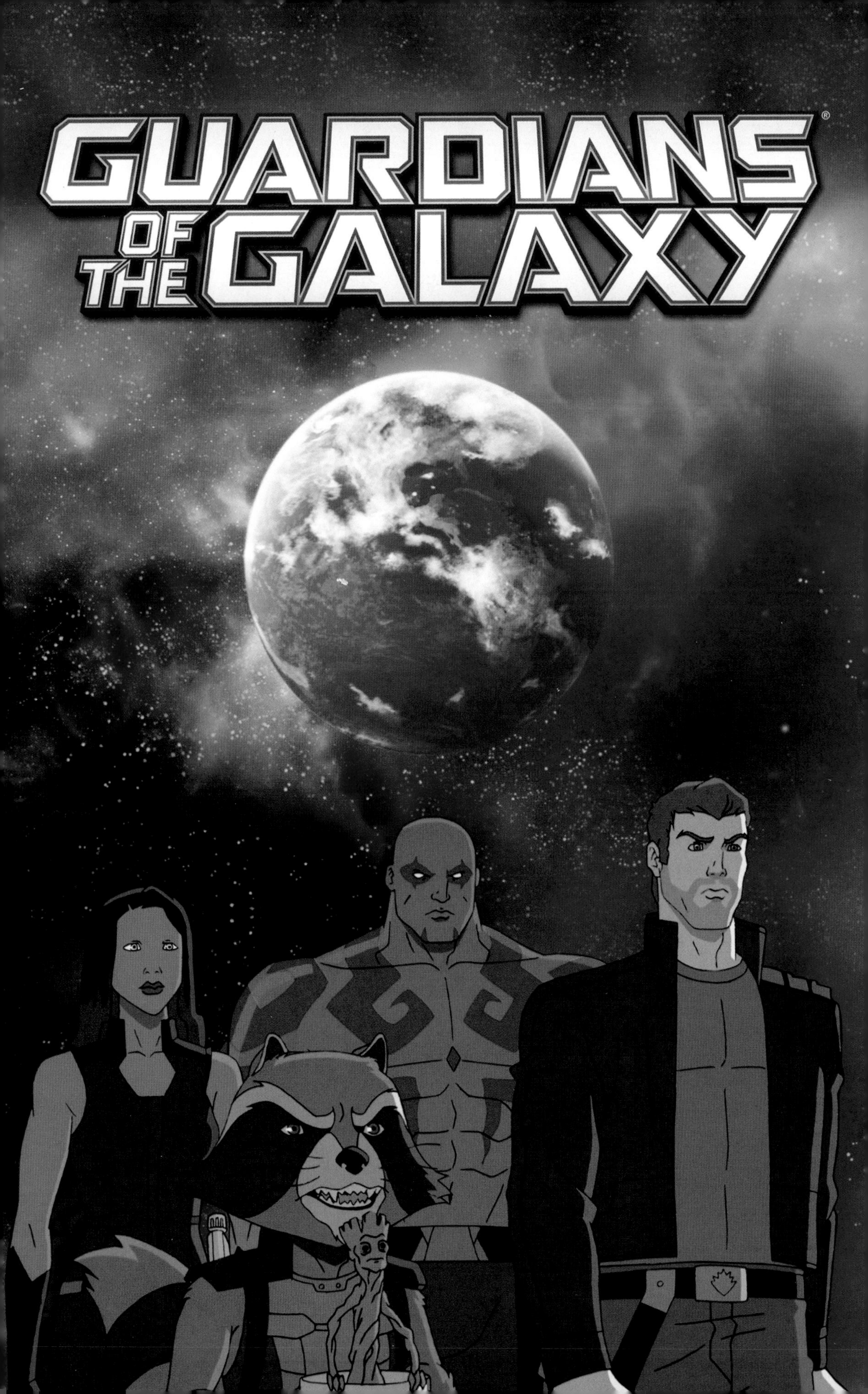
GUARDIANS® OF THE GALAXY

GUARDIANS OF THE GALAXY

COLLECT THEM ALL!

Set of 6 Hardcover Books ISBN: 978-1-5321-4069-3

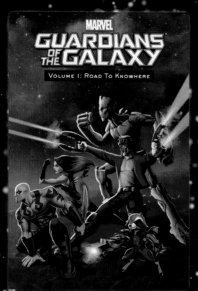

**Hardcover Book ISBN
978-1-5321-4070-9**

**Hardcover Book ISBN
978-1-5321-4071-6**

**Hardcover Book ISBN
978-1-5321-4072-3**

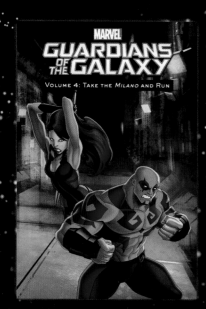

**Hardcover Book ISBN
978-1-5321-4073-0**

**Hardcover Book ISBN
978-1-5321-4074-7**

**Hardcover Book ISBN
978-1-5321-4075-4**